THE YORKSHIRE MISFIT

The Dales Will Never Be The Same Again!

C K Lobb

THE YORKSHIRE MISFIT

City girl, turned country bumpkin Jess, is no stranger to life's ups and downs. Now in her mid thirties, and not the slightest bit concerned about settling down, she decides to go it alone in the Yorkshire Dales, working as a self employed rural farm secretary. Her character can perhaps best be described as James Herriot meets Bridget Jones.

Some may call her difficult, some may call her feisty, others may see her as a bit of a stubborn, non-conformist but Jess is ok with being all of those things as she is no stranger to having to walk her own path without apology. Now at an age where she is less likely to give folk the benefit of the doubt, you are about to take a peek through the amusing daily lens that Jess cares to call her life, set in the rugged Yorkshire Dales

I would like to dedicate this book to my sister, Sharon Lobb and her partner John Perkins, who rescued me one night from a fate that I thankfully shall never know. Also to my friend and proof reader, Kelda Yeo and finally to my beloved and closest companion, my rescue Border Collie, Flint.

"Personally I think happiness is highly over rated and I actually prefer the misery that life throws at you. It's more familiar to us up here in Yorkshire. We don't need happiness, just a strong cup of Builders Tea and a slap on the back and we're good to go".

CONTENTS

Title Page	1
THE YORKSHIRE MISFIT	2
Dedication	3
Copyright	6
THE STOP TAP	7
THE BREAKDOWN	10
MISSION IMPOSSIBLE	13
THE COW WHISPERER	16
THE PERFECT PATIENT	18
THE GREAT ESCAPE	21
DENIAL AND THE RATS	23

COPYRIGHT

This book or any portion thereof may not be reproduced or used without the express written permission of the author or publisher. The author and publisher assume no responsibility from any errors or omissions or any coincidental similarities to events, situations or persons detailed within this publication. No liability is assumed from any detail contained within.

Editor/Author: C K Lobb
Proofreader: Kelda Yeo
Interior Design: C K Lobb

ISBN: 9781076620033
Imprint: Independently published
Have A Laugh A Day Series – Book One

All Rights Reserved.
© 2019 C K Lobb

THE STOP TAP

*"The thing is you know where you are with a frown
but a smile can hide a thousand lies."*

❖ ❖ ❖

It all started off so well with the house move. Just the white goods to move out and all will be well in the world. But alas, this is my world where common sense never prevails and smoothness is usually the last item on the agenda. Today wasn't about to disappoint. The removal guy and my friend, whom we shall call Robert, because well, that's his name; moved the washing machine away from the pipe work. Robert suddenly turns to me,
"What's that hissing noise? Can you hear any hissing?" He leans further in towards the pipe.
"Oh no, it's not a gas leak is it?" I asked in complete alarm.

Suddenly water bolts aggressively out of the pipe at such a force he almost falls backward with the sheer strength of it. He quickly clambers back up, wipes the water from his face and proceeds to place both hands over the pipe only to discover that it just spews out from each side. He turns to me, his face and hair already covered with water droplets hanging from his hairline.
"Where's the tap?" he yells.
"Well they're there silly, on top of the sink. Where'd you think they are?" I roll my eyes.............men!
"No the stop tap. Where's the stop tap?"
I look at him and frown. "What's a stop tap?" I shout, shrugging my shoulders and holding my hands out to the side.

The world for that moment stopped turning. Even the water seemed to stop spewing out of the pipe in amazement at the naivety of the question. My friend looks back at me with the most hopeless, confused, desperate stare. Surely I knew what a stop tap was? Nope, not me! I shake my head from side to side.
The removal guy starts grinning. I don't know what he's so happy about, grinning and whistling away for the last hour. I'm not paying him that much. You know, I'm highly suspicious of people who appear too happy. Personally I think happiness is highly over rated and I actually prefer the misery that life throws at you. It's more familiar to us up north. In Yorkshire we don't need happiness, just a strong cup of Builders Tea and a slap on the back and we're good to go. The thing is you know where you are with a frown but a smile can hide a thousand lies.

The removal guy reassuringly pats me on the shoulder.

"It's all right darling. You're not supposed to know, you're just a woman!" He smiles smugly and then wait for it. He winks. See now in my world that's just plain fighting talk. He has actually managed to respect and demean me in the same sentence and he doesn't even know it. Now I'm not going to say that they don't make men like they used to because that would clearly be wrong. I mean let's face it, they've not been made that good for a long time now. So instead I smile my sweetest smile, lean in and say,

"Firstly, honey bun, stop calling me darling. Secondly, what's wrong with your eye, got a twitch and thirdly would you put that tape measure down before I wrap it round your dangly bits!" You see, this is the thing; we don't need political world leaders to sort out sexism in Yorkshire. No, we just need to adopt a strong, forceful Yorkshire, nay Lancashire lass to set the record straight. And there you go. Problem solved!

"Could you two swop pleasantries later, we've got a crisis going on here," yells Robert.

Robert, who is completely dressed in black and wet through from head to toe, is mysteriously beginning to resemble a male stripper. Wow, I've never noticed that before! All we need now is a fireman's pole and we could earn some serious cash to help pay for all this water damage.

In a last ditch desperate attempt to stop the spurge of water, Robert defiantly points his index finger towards the pipe and shoves it into the pipe work. This worked for half a second until the water hit him at force in his eyes. Well that was it for me, I felt like laughing and crying at the same time but I kept my dignity intact by observing the delivery driver's backside as he bent over the sink. His underpants read "I'M THE MAN." Really? Well if he has to advertise the fact, he surely must be. It wasn't a pretty sight I can tell you.

Suddenly, Robert quickly disappears upstairs.
"It might be upstairs...........the tap!" I hear the thud........ thud..........thud........ thud as his wet shoes hit every step as he leaps up the stairs and then suddenly I hear him fall, his backside hitting every single step as he bob sledges down the carpeted stairs only to land in a cluttered, bundled heap at my feet.
"What happened?" I cried. The water is rising. "Somebody make the water stop," I shout. Even the removal guy is sweating now which is a first considering he was a snail in his previous life and is still under that influence in the present one.
"I think I've broke my backside. There's no grip on that stair carpet you know," yelps Robert.

I knew I should have got better carpet on my stairs but I get that from my Dad. He was always wanting to save money. We got new carpet once in our house as kids and from that point on we had to walk upstairs with our feet only touching the perimeter of the carpet on each step. You know, to avoid wear and tear in the middle. After a few years though Dad spotted wear and tear marks showing on the carpet so in absolute alarm he applied for a Stair Master in the hope he could prolong the life of the carpet by faking a disability. It turned out that he didn't have to fake it as his hips and knees were so knackered from all the strange stair step routine that he got his Stair Master in the end. He would have jumped for joy .... if only he could! He was full of great ideas like that. Well until he passed away that is and then all we had left were our memories and bowlegs by our early twenties. All the neighbours thought that our family had been inflicted with Rickets. Not true, we were simply passionate about our carpets.

Anyway, I opened a cupboard door in the kitchen and spotted.............a stop tap!
"There's a tap here," I yell out.

"No I've done that one," shouts the removal guy.
"No look there's another underneath!" I shout back.
"Turn it," Robert yells. "Turn it................turn it!"
So I did. The water stopped and we all just stand looking at each other with ripples of water playfully stroking our ankles. Complete utter silence. Silence except for the sound of lapping water hugging our ankles.
"So there were two stop taps then," muses the removal guy. "I must have turned the dummy one."
"For Pete's sake! You are the dummy one," I snapped.
"Ey, you didn't even know what a stop tap was.................and I'm called John."
"Ey, I'm just a woman. I'm not supposed to know what a stop tap is remember!" I snort back.
"Can you two give it a rest. I'm going home," says Robert defeated.
"You're not getting in my van like that. You're wet through," grins John.
"Wait! I've got a plan!" I gleefully yell.

One minute later, Robert emerges wearing nothing except his boots and the removal guy's hi-viz jacket that comes to just above his knees. His wet clothes rolled under his arms. Chippendales out! Full Monty in!

Unfortunately the police were out with their speed camera on the A65 and you know what I'm going to say next don't you? The police asked them both to step out of the vehicle but Robert respectably refused on the grounds that he was naked and had a sore bottom. I promised Robert faithfully that I would never ever repeat this story to save any local embarrassment but unfortunately they don't make women like they used to either. So I lied!

THE BREAKDOWN

'CAN YOU CROSS THIS FIELD IN 10 SECONDS? OUR BULL CAN!'

◆ ◆ ◆

So there I was, stuck on the lay-by on a quiet county lane having broken down. I was on my way to see a new customer at a local farm. I was pretty confident that I could fix the tyre myself, being the confident independent woman that I am, and more specifically because I have the RAC on speed dial. I'm suddenly interrupted by someone whom I presume is the driver of the tractor, who's engine I could hear rumbling away, very close by.
"Well well well; what do we have here then?" he hollowed.

I spot a pair of un-matching wellies at my feet and look up to discover a figure that I can only describe as a descendent of Worzel Gummidge. Unfortunately however, there was no sign of Aunt Sally with a nice cup of tea which I could really do with right now. It was the orange bailer twine being used as a belt to hold up his trousers which caused me the greatest concern on so many levels, but I tried to maintain a friendly and cordial approach. He was clearly the local farmer, his tractor just by the gate.
"Well," I smiled sarcastically "I'd say it was a flat tyre but what do I know I'm just a mere female." I laughed and he didn't. That, there and then, was my first warning sign. That was my cue. My cue to run fast and far and never look back! But did I? Nope! Why not? Because I'm Jess and I like as much stress and hardship in my life as humanly possible!
"Aye, you're not wrong there lass. It's a flat tyre all right."
"Go away," I responded sarcastically, "d'you think?" I grinned. Again nothing. So there it was. My second cue to escape. Did I take it? Nope. It's me and clearly I completely ignore blatantly obvious signs that I'm entering twilight zone territory.
"D'you have black tongue on that thing," he asked pointing to my mobile.
"Black tongue? You don't mean blue tooth do you?"
"Aye, that's what I said lass. Right I'll just get this sign up and I'll thee a lift."
"Oh no really, I'm fine. I can manage......I........"
"No you can't manage. You're a mere woman like you just said," he interrupted.

See now this guy is starting to tick me off. So he had heard me! He struts off across the lane and I have to say that I've never seen anyone strut confidently off into the distance whilst wearing bailer twine as a belt and cow poop all over his trousers, but this guy manages to pull it off quite nicely. He has this kind of cocky arrogance about him which some people may politely call 'quietly confident.' Me, I'd rather say he's probably the kind of bloke whom I think would take quite some time to get off any high horse if you know what I'm saying. I too take my time with high horses but I have particularly short legs and that's the excuse I'm sticking to. Plus what us shorties lack in height, we make up for in leverage. Not only that, we have to make a stance otherwise you'd only get tall people in positions of power and I can't talk to tall people because well, they hurt my neck.

"Right well, I'll get this sign up then..........for the bull," he shouts, pulling a sign post from his tractor.
"Bull?...............what bull?..............where?" As you can see I'm very comfortable around bulls.
"Well," he said, "our bull keeps chasing folk and they've started to complain about it so I'm just sorting him out now."
"Oh God, you're not gonna let him out are you?" I cry.
"No nothing like that. I'm just trying to educate the public that's all," he grinned. At last a bit of sense. Maybe he's not that bad after all. He pulls a can of spray paint from his pockets, shakes it, grins back at me and starts spraying a message on the sign. I look at my watch. He starts whistling. Time is passing on. Geez, how long does it take to write KEEP OUT? And then he shows me the sign.
"There you go lass - that should sort 'em out!"

It reads – '***CAN YOU CROSS THIS FIELD IN 10 SECONDS? OUR BULL CAN!***'

I realise at this point that this is no ordinary farmer. I've met ordinary farmers before. Yes a tad eccentric maybe, often loners, sometimes very sociable animals but this guy clearly makes the rules as he goes along. It's like he is living in his own world where he gets to make all the rules and they all look completely normal but the problem is they only look normal to him. You see, he's a bit like Trump except with honesty, sincerity and a lot more bailer twine.
"You can't put that up! It's hardly a normal sign is it?" I shout.
"Well that depends on what you mean by normal lass," he grinned.

And that's when it hit me. When you ask someone a question about what's normal and they start to debate the meaning of that very word, you just know there is gonna be trouble ahead. Because the truth is, they know they're not normal. You know they're not normal, and they know, that you know, they're not normal. Heck! How the hell do I get out of this one? But instead of getting out, I get more and more reeled in. In fact if someone offered me a rather large spade right now, I'm sure I couldn't dig my way any deeper into this messy situation. So much so that he ends up offering me a lift and I accept! Yes, you heard me!

So there I was sat in the tractor, accepting a lift off Farmer Trump.
"Does it not have a seat belt?" I joked.
"You can share mine with me if you want lass." He grinned; a broad toothless grin and started up the noisy engine. It was at that very moment that I realised the enormity of the mistake I was making. We were now moving. I turned to the widow grimacing and uttered the words,
"I think I'd feel safer with Satan."
"What's that you say?" he shouted over the engine.
I said, "I think I'm a safe 'un................... Can't this thing go any faster? I'm late already." I shout.
"Well I would do but the brakes are a bit temperamental you see."
"What do you mean a bit temperamental?" I stutter.

"Well they don't always work so I have to slow her down steady like."
Panic!
"Hang on, what's that you just said?"
"I said I have to slow her down steady like," he yells.
"No……. No ……the first bit……," I shout back.
"I said the brakes don't work…….see."
He pumps the pedal up and down madly and absolutely nothing happens.
"See, told ya," he grins proudly.

He looked positively ecstatic at this point and I knew there and then I was actually dealing with madness. Yes he may look normal if you deduct the bailer twine and I truly know we must never judge by looks but we should always………. always………. judge by bailer twine. Plus I don't know why he keeps referring to the tractor as SHE but I have a feeling it has something to do with men thinking women are temperamental due to hormones but please, nobody is ruled more by their hormones more than men so I'm not buying that one for starters.

The tractor is now speeding along the country lanes driven by a farmer with only bailer twine holding up his trousers, with brakes that don't work and a driver that is clearly somewhat of a mental question mark. It seemed like a lifetime but we eventually arrive at our destination. Never has the grating of a handbrake sounded so beautiful. I almost tumble out of the tractor, completely missing the steps down to the ground stinking of diesel, cow poop and engine oil. I'm out! I'm free! Never ever again will I accept a lift from Farmer Trump over there. I'm just happy to be here in one piece. I hammer the farmhouse door with my fist. The lady of the house answers. I grab her hand and look at her desperately waiting for her to offer me into her home and pour me any form of alcoholic beverage on offer to help steady my nerves. I'm almost breathless and don't really know what I'm saying. "It's me…….secretary …………..here safely and soundly." I heave a sigh of relief and hold out my shaking hand. She looks at my bedraggled appearance, eyeing me up and down suspiciously before placing a delicate finger below her nose.

"I think you've got the wrong day love, we're not expecting you till next Sunday. We're all just out for the day." I stare blankly, speechless. Yes that's right, me……speechless! Never fear though, my right hand man suddenly appears by my side. He puts his arm around me and gives me a pat on the shoulder.
"Not to worry lass, you can get a lift back with me!" I let out a whimper. "But don't worry," he continues, "we'll be much quicker coz its downhill all the way." Right, that's it. I've just died and gone to bailer twine hell!

MISSION IMPOSSIBLE

"Oh yes, this is now a military operation of the finest order. Operation Mayhem is about to commence."

❖ ❖ ❖

What is this fascination with shopping? I hate shopping, especially for clothes. I think the reason why I hate shopping is because everyone else looks so happy doing it and I cannot for the life of me fathom out why. I mean really what is so interesting? Besides, I've always considered it untrendy to be well……….trendy! Well today the shopping list was simple. It simply read 'one pair of jeans.' Sounds simple enough, yes?

To get me through this, an absolute steadfast focus and a military style approach is essential to undertake this particular operation. Oh yes, this is now a military operation of the finest order. Operation Mayhem is about to commence. I stand in the car park having secured my vehicle. My watch and all mobile devices have been synchronised-check. Mobile phone switched on-check. Purse-check! Shopping list-check! Whistle-check! That's in case of in store violence. Well, it is discount day for the over 60's! I should really be wearing my combat trousers for this type of mission but that may be a bit over the top. Oh no, did I pack my infra-red night goggles. Yep!-check!

Now if only there were just one kind of jeans to choose from but no, that would be far too easy because these days we like choice. We like long, skinny, boot cut, low rise, wide leg, boyfriend, cropped, high rise, casual etc. Bloody hell they're jeans! When did this all get so complicated? This is not a good start. I realise that I will need to try at least 4 different sizes of each style, 8, 10, 12 and 14 because that's the crazy world we live in now. With an eagle eye, operating efficiently and swiftly, I precisely target 4 different styles of jeans and 4 sizes of each and quickly stuff them into my basket. Note that's 16 pairs in total. Affirmative! My shopping basket weighs a ton and I've got a major sweat on starting already, so now I'm feeling less like an eagle and more like a sitting duck. However onwards and upwards.

As if on some form of assault course, dodging prams, overtaking groups of teenagers and giving the over 60s club a very wide birth, I eventually make it over to the changing rooms. The eagle has landed. Over!

There is a changing room assistant waving me into the next available cubicle who is teetering on the highest pair of wedged shoes imaginable. Anyway, in I go, locking the changing room door. Operation Mayhem has begun! I stare at the overflowing basket and heave a heavy sigh. I look at my watch and set the timer. Ok, so it's 30 seconds per item, 5 seconds getting them on, 5 seconds getting them off and the other 20 is for looks, general fit and not to forget sitting down in them. Ok, slight problem already. There is no chair so I'm just going to have to hover within a seated position like I do when I have to use a public toilet but I've got strong thighs, I can handle it. Now then speed and precision is of the upmost importance otherwise the momentum is lost. Here goes. I'm going in!

There are never enough spare hangers in these changing rooms so to increase speed and ease I thought I'd just drop them to the floor and put them all back on their hangers at the end. I'm actually trying to be efficient. Or is that deficient? I'm not quite sure. Things are starting to get a little bleary. Within minutes, I'd formulated a great system. I decide on 3 piles. The definitely not, the maybe and the yes pile. So there I was ………Too big. (Damn!) Too short. (Bollocks!) Too long. (Bloody hell fire!) Too small. (Sweet mother of Mary!) The pressure is starting to get to me. The 'yes' pile is empty, the 'maybe' pile has one pair of 'relaxed' jeans but that's only because I like the word relax, and the 'no' pile is continuing to grow.

I'm now getting to the end of the 16 pairs and I'm almost hyperventilating with disbelief. Not a single pair fit. Not a single, bloody pair! I then get to the very last pair. Well this is it, that's two hours of my life that I'm never going to get back. I don't know why I'm even bothering trying this last pair on. But wait! Oh my God, these are perfect, they fit brilliantly. Not too tight or loose. Not too short or long. It's a miracle. They're amazing! They're brilliant! Crap, they're mine! They're the ones I came in with! Oh for the love of God! I look at the pile of jeans on the floor. So this is shopping is it? Well, isn't this just dandy! What fun! Such a joy!

The denim mountain at my feet look back at me and I actually feel sorry for them along with the tired looking coat hangers by their side, looking quite lonely and naked without their clothes on. They offered such hope on the coat hanger but now they are resorted to a mere pile of rags on the floor. I put my hands on my hips and sigh. How the hell am I going to get all these jeans back onto their rightful coat hangers? It's going to take forever and a day! This is becoming pain staking and utterly overwhelming. Suddenly, like some almighty power from beyond, three words immediately spring to my mind – 'Abort the mission!' Affirmative!

I thought I'd better evacuate before somebody spots the carnage. I slowly open the changing room door. I wait a few minutes until the coast is clear and there is no sign of the wedges queen. Yes, the coast is clear. The eagle is on the move. Unfortunately, the only way I can now exit is back through the tills.

As I wait at the tills trying to find an opportunity to casually wander through, I see a small crowd of staff congregating at the till nearest to me. They are looking disgruntled.
"It's such as mess in there. Jeans everywhere. Coat hangers in a huge pile all mixed up." As the other folk in the queue were also getting involved in this, I thought I had better join in, you know so as to blend in.
"Wow, that's terrible," I say, shaking my head in disbelief with the over 60's club. "Well, I blame the youth of today, I really do. No discipline you see." They all nod in agreement. As we are talking away, I see the 'wedges' assistant charging her way towards me with a face like thunder, armed with about 20 coat hangers. Oh…Oh…..this is now developing into a code red situation. I repeat, a code red! I am now panicking as she gets nearer. Oh no, here come the anxiety sweats. I just need my sugar levels to

drop now and that's it, I've had it. Once these two kick in together, I seriously go weak and will have no choice but to crawl out on all 4 fours in a bid to get to my car. Admittedly this will slow me down somewhat but will certainly get the interest of the dog sat patiently outside, waiting for its owner. As she gets closer, I find I am frozen to the spot in sheer panic. Suddenly, by a stroke of luck, she trips. She appears to have fallen off her shoes. This is my chance.

As everyone runs one way to help her, I run like crazy, in the opposite direction, out of the store and straight to my car. I'm red faced, my heart is racing, I'm out of breath and I can't feel my legs but I have a huge grin on my face. So this is shopping is it? Well, you know what, I kind of enjoyed it. I might even come back tomorrow. Operation Mayhem: The Sequel. Over and out!

THE COW WHISPERER

"I smile my most sickly smile. It's well perfected when dealing with the male of the species."

◆ ◆ ◆

So there I was, out jogging on the country lanes. Just me and my nice new trainers on a lovely, warm sunny afternoon. I turned a corner and suddenly came across about 10 cows just standing randomly in the middle of the country lane. I looked up and down the lane, not a single soul to be seen. I noticed the gate where they had clearly come from, slightly open. It's no wonder farmers despair of the general public not shutting field gates behind them. How irresponsible. Well, this was clearly a time for action. These cows definitely look like they need my help and I wasn't about to abandon them in the middle of the lane. I don't know why I like cows so much? Maybe it's because no matter how fast the world turns, they continue to go at their own pace regardless. It's like they've given two fingers up to the rest of the world. I quite respect that!

Anyway, I adopted my expert cow moving skills (basically waving my arms in the air and hissing) to get them back into the field safely. They stared at me blankly for a bit as if they thought I was trying to take off and then suddenly, as if by magic, I appear to be getting through. They actually start turning around and like a falling American wave, they all follow suit back into the field. Hey, look at me. I'm quite the herdswoman. Wow, I'm really good at this. Perhaps folk will now call me the cow whisperer. It's as if the cows know I'm helping them. You know, I'm so good with animals. Maybe I'll be in demand for turning cattle, who knows. Maybe one woman and her cows award. Oh yes, I can almost smell the shit!

I notice that there are even a few cars waiting patiently till I'm done with my herding talents. Wow, I'm now even holding up traffic but as I look to be in complete control the drivers quite happily sit and wait. I close the gate proudly and beckon to the drivers to drive on steadfast within my professional capacity for all things four legged. There was a bloke, mid thirties, sitting in his van which read, *'Delivering Excellence Since 1932.'* I was about to tell him he was looking good for his age but he got to me first!

"Not bad work that, you know, for a woman," he joked, winking. See now, there's always one smarty pants never too far away isn't there? I smile my most sickly smile. It's well perfected when dealing with the male of the species. Often it's combined with a good dollop of sarcasm and a sprinkle of wind up material.

"Well, I'll go out on a limb and class that as compliment," I snigger. "Eh, and you're not a bad driver, you know, considering your a fella." I too wink back. Ever done that to a bloke? Try it! They find it utterly confusing due to what we politely call 'social norms' or in other words, caveman territory-! Silence! No words! Nothing! Non- comprendez! Well my motto is, if you snooze you lose and this guy can't react quick enough so he's definitely snoozing. I turn away and waltz off down the lane.

Speaking of men. I went on a blind date the other night. We went to a restaurant and all was going well until, can you believe it, he decides to reach for a calculator at the end of the meal. Oh and did I mention, the restaurant was McDonalds? Oh and did I mention, that we went through the drive through? Oh and did I mention, that's me done for another decade?

Now then, the cows. They are still looking bemused with all the fuss and attention. I bet they..........I suddenly stop, mid sentence. Now hang one cotton picking minute, those udders look pretty damn full and then like a bolt of lightning, it suddenly hit me. Something made me turn to face the other side of the lane and it wasn't women's intuition. I know that for sure as I don't possess it. I mean, I am female, well as far as I know, but I think I was at the back of the queue when femininity and insight was being handed out. Clearly, the sign was from the farmer. It read: *'Cows crossing - drive slowly!'* Blinkin Eck! The cow whisperer has only just gone and turned the cows back into the field when they were actually crossing the road to be milked. But where was the farmer? Suddenly I heard the sound of a quad bike in the distance. I turned back towards the gate, the cows staring at me inquisitively. I looked beyond the cows to see a quad bike coming over the horizon with more cows just in front of it heading towards me. Shit! I looked back to the cows still staring at me and noted their udders again. Yep they were still full! These cows were on their way to be milked and I've just put them all back in the field again. Oh my God! Panic is setting in as the quad bike is getting nearer. The farmer now no longer in a seated position on his bike by the way, probably wondering what the hell was going on. The cows were now congregating at the closed gate and were seemingly very excited with this new milking method. Sweet mother of Mary, how the hell do I get out of this one?

In panic I turn back toward the gate and attempt to kick it open. Firstly I forget that I have my new, SOFT trainers on and not my walking boots. Ouch! Second, the cow whisperer had secured the gate 10 seconds ago so why is she now kicking it? Call me a pessimist but I get the distinct feeling that my herdswoman of the year award has gone for a burton!
Damn it! No time to think! Panic! Horror! So how does this story end I hear you cry? Did I open the gate and patiently wait for the farmer to explain my behaviour? Nope. Did I manage to open the gate and lead the cows politely across the lane to assist? Nope. I simply did what any self respecting, interfering, non gate shutting member of the public would do..... I took off down the lane as fast as my new trainers could carry me. Sorry Mr farmer!

However the good news is that on route, further up the lane, I spot some white fluffy things in the distance. My finely tuned animal instincts tell me that they are sheep and in my expert opinion they look like they definitely need some assistance. You can't just leave them in the middle of the lane on their own like that, they need rescuing. Right I'll just nip home, get my Border Collie and give him a whirl with the sheep. One man, ney woman and her dog, here I come!

THE PERFECT PATIENT

"I am relaxed, what makes you think I'm not relaxed. I couldn't be more relaxed. Gosh it's hot in here. Is it hot in here?"

◆ ◆ ◆

So there I was, sat in the waiting room at the doctors. All I really want to do is blend in and be ignored but have you not noticed that when you keep yourself to yourself, folk become more interested in you? It's true. Just the other day this bloke said that he'd heard I was a nice person. I told him that he really shouldn't listen to rumours. Bingo! More interest! That's the secret ladies. Don't give a damn.

So here I was trying the same approach at the doctors. Just chilling, it's no big deal, it's just a neee...... oh God, I can't even say the word needle. Am I sweating? Yes my palms are sweating just at the very word. How the hell am I gonna get through this blood test? The problem is, the more I try and stop thinking about needles the more I start thinking about needles. It's very rare now that needles get stuck in veins, so they say, but just yesterday I won a free coupon for teabags at the till and I never win anything so I'm beating some odds already and that ain't good. Gosh I hope my nurse isn't twelve. What if she has only just finished her training and I'm her first real patient?

No, it's no good. I need to get out of here fast. I mean I've done well. I've made the first step. I've exposed myself to the fear and now I need to run and hide as my reward. I grab my bag and attempt my get away. Suddenly the nurse appears and shouts my name. I look up pretending I hadn't heard her and looked about the waiting room as innocently as I could muster. Perhaps if I say nothing she will go away! The problem is I was at least 20 years younger than anyone else in the room and if I was called Betty, Ethel or Doris I could have easily made my escape but the nurse is no fool and looks straight at me. Are you Jess? My mouth opens but there are no words. She looks at me and raises an eyebrow.

"Are you playing dumb?" she grins. I assured her that I wasn't and that I always look like this.
"Er, I think I may have to lie down for this needle," I say.
"You're not nervous are you?" she mused.
"Me! Nervous? Ha............as if. I just thought you might be nervous. Are you nervous because if this is your first time I'd rather come back when you're a bit more experienced. The thing is; you only look young to me. How old are you by the way?"

She stares at me, bemused.
"I'm sixty two. Take your jacket off please. Been here 30 years love. Roll up your sleeve please."

You know, I'm not too sure that I like this no nonsense approach but that was the least of my worries right now. She then mentions that she needs to go and get a strap to help locate my veins. The mistake she made, besides mentioning the word strap to help locate a vein, was leaving the room to actually go and get said strap as this was my ideal opportunity to mentally note any exits in order to make my escape.

If there is an open window, I will definitely be going through it. And at this practice that's easy peasy as its all on one level, unlike the last practice when I escaped from the second floor. The sheets that I used from the bed that day merely served as a harness, if you will, and aside from a fractured ankle, broken wrist and some minor internal bleeding all was well. Not to mention that it was a perfect opportunity to work on my fear of heights, so don't try telling me that I don't face my fears!

I noticed, to my alarm, there were no exits and it was at this precise moment that my claustrophobia decides to kick in. I take a deep breath. I find myself licking my forefinger and holding it into the air whilst a finger on my other hand is holding in one of my nostrils. I take a deep breath, Yes, yes I think there is enough air in the room so I'm fine at the moment. Don't panic. Stay calm. I peer towards the tray she has assembled. My brain is saying DONT LOOK but my eyes are completely ignoring my brain. It's as if they have a mind of their own.

Anyway I glance down at my arm and back to the needle on the tray. Now either that's one large needle or I've got very skinny arms. I'm going with the latter as that's the only way I'm gonna get out of here in one piece and with my dignity intact. OK forget dignity. Just getting out in one piece will suit me just dandy.

That's it. I'm out of here. I get up and bend down to get my bag, meanwhile the nurse comes back in.
"So how are we doing?" I shoot back up and lean casually on the bed.
"Oh I'm fine, couldn't be better." I find myself yawning you know to appear casual and care free. The problem is my jaw is that tense that I can barely close it again. Gosh all I need now is to start drooling!
"Now just relax," she insists.
"I am relaxed, what makes you think I'm not relaxed. I couldn't be more relaxed. Gosh it's hot in here. Is it hot in here?"
"I think it's best if you lie down for this in case you get dizzy," she assures me. Now then, just the mere suggestion of getting dizzy makes me feel, well..............dizzy.
"Ok then so it's just an overall check today," she said.
"Oh that sounds good then. Yes, check the old engine. The old MOT. The..........gosh is that the needle? It looks a bit large. So it's just the one needle then is it?"
"That's right, just one needle," she nods.
"Phew, one needle. I can just about cope with....."
"And three bottles," she interrupts. I stop and freeze. I slowly turn to her.
"Sorry, did you just say bottles. You know, as in more than one?"
"That's right, I said three bottles," she confidently assures me.
Well that was it then, a needle fine. Bottle perhaps a bit fine. Bottles plural......... definitely not fine! There is now good news and bad news. The good news is I suddenly don't have the problem with the word needle. The bad news is that I now have a problem with the word bottles.

She shows me the bottles. This is supposed to make me feel better.

"They're not that big," she smiles unconvincingly. But you know what folks, neither am I!

"You've got good veins," she adds.

Oh! Oh! Now I've gone and got a problem with the word veins. My problem words are started to fill up and I should be mentally filing them away in the 'Words That Scare Me' file but actually that file is beginning to get pretty full. I'm beginning to get desperate and so I try bargaining tactics, always the last resort of the fear process before fight or flight kicks in.

"Could you not just take half the amount and then I'll come back and give the other half next time. Say one and a half bottles?"

"No," she says.

"Could you not just take one sample and gather all the tests from that one sample then?"

"No," she repeats.

Ok, I'm feeling that this particular sister of mercy is not into bargaining and I'm starting to lose faith in her ability to accommodate my fears.

So there I was lying down, sleeves rolled up, sweating like a pig in a bacon factory knowing that I'm about to be………. I can't even say it……injected. And then came the magical words, like music to my ears!

"All done," she says.

Really? Wow! I didn't feel a thing. She is good. I take a few seconds and breath. That wasn't bad at all. I get up slowly.

"I thought I did really well there but what can I say, I'm a natural. I mean after all it's only a needle."

She smiles at me and then turns her back to use the computer. I get up slowly.

"You know, I think I could have made a good nurse don't you?"

"Close the door on your way out won't you dear," she said adamantly.

You know I liked her. And I get the feeling that she liked me. I can tell when someone likes me. They tend to struggle to look me in the eye you know and erm…….well communicate but that's likely due to the fact that I've got a strong character. I know this to be true because I'm a people person at heart. Well you know, within reason. As long as they don't talk to me, don't look at me, and give me a very wide birth I think people are great. You know I hope I get her again next time. I liked her and I bet she feels exactly the same way about me. Now then, off to the dentist next. Gosh I hope that dental hygienist knows how to use that scraper thing properly. I wonder how they get qualified? I hope I'm not their first patient ………

THE GREAT ESCAPE

"Right now sis, remember when we pass through supermarket security, try and look normal, ok!"

◆ ◆ ◆

Ok so picture this if you will. Imagine a completely empty supermarket car park on a very early Sunday morning. You get out of bed; meet up with your sister, just so you can both grace the aisles in complete peace without other folk getting in the way. The store is seconds away from opening their doors to a completely peaceful Sunday morning, stress free, shopping experience. Sounds good so far, yes?

We are parked in the car park and the fact that there are tons of empty car parking spaces around me is a very important thing to remember in this story. Suddenly another 'shopper' pulls up in the space right bedsides mine. Not only do they park in the space to my immediate right but let's just say I'd be lucky if I could get a sheet of paper between our two wing mirrors. I turn to view an elderly lady driving some large, silver monstrosity which will no doubt compromise this, and the next generation's supply of clean air but eh, she doesn't care, she is clearly living for the now!

The supermarket doors suddenly open. She spots them and bolts out of her car like a 16 year old on his first date. I open my car door only to realise that I can't get out as my next door neighbour has clearly abandoned her car to enjoy the delights of stress free Sunday morning shopping whilst I'm now trapped in my vehicle. After about 15 seconds of struggling to get out whilst I get redder and redder in the face my sister says,

"Look why don't you just drive into another space, then you'll have loads of room. Or I'll get out and you just crawl through this side!"

I look at her blankly. Damn! I hadn't thought of doing that. So now I need to back track. In other words; lie.

"Well obviously, duh………..but why should I have to move? Beside I would prefer doing it my way thank you very much."

She shakes her head, grins smugly, folds her arms and leans back in the chair like your mates used to do at school when you were getting told off by a teacher. Plus I admit this would have been an excellent plan ten seconds ago but now my backside and legs are out of the vehicle with only my upper body remaining so I figure I'm half way there already. Plus my backside is the biggest obstacle and if that can get through this narrow gap the rest will follow quite happily. She is still grinning at me.

"I know you're finding this entertaining," I mutter between breaths. Almost there ......yes......yes......I'm out......I'm free..... I'm free! I snatch my first clear breath of freedom on the outside of the vehicle. I've never felt frustration and happiness simultaneously before but this was definitely one of those rare moments.

Having now escaped, I was sweating, red faced and looking like I'd been dragged through a hedge backwards. I wander round the posh car like a wild cat stalking its prey.

"Clearly one exhaust pipe isn't enough," I shout to my sister.

Anyway the delights of early, Sunday morning shopping await and I've wasted enough time on the great escape to waste any more seconds on folk who enjoy invading my space and polluting the environment.

So there we were, in store, shopping away. My sister has gone down one aisle and I was leaning over my trolley to grab a box of cornflakes. Suddenly I hear this crackling upper class voice,

"You do realise that you're blocking the aisle with your trolley don't you. It's really so inconsiderate as I cannot get past but I suppose that's your generation isn't it!" I turned round - guess who? I take a deep breath, bite my bottom lip and smile my most sarcastic smile.

"Well I am sooooooooo sorry. How rude and utterly thoughtless it was of me to block you in," I gasp, purposely unconvincingly.

I immediately grab my trolley and defiantly strut off down the aisle. My sister managed to calm me down and insisted that we carry on with our 'peaceful, stress free, Sunday morning shopping' experience! Suddenly there is an in store public announcement.

'This is a customer announcement - could all customers please check the whereabouts of their trolleys and return any that do not belong to them. A customer is currently waiting at reception for the return of their goods. Thank you.'

I promptly turn to my sister, grinning.

"Ey I tell you what sis, there's some sad people about eh! Fancy walking off with someone else's trolley! I mean, how stupid must you have to be to do that!" I laughed and then caught my sister's eye. At that very moment, as if some mysterious mystic forces were at play, we both suddenly stopped and looked at each other with absolute dread. We simultaneously veer our eyes down into our trolley and discover the worst. Oh no, there wasn't a single item in there that we recognised. I must have confidently strutted off with the double exhaust pipes trolley! Blinkin' Eck! What now?

So what happened next? Did we return the trolley? What and have to face the exhaust pipe lady? No way! Did we go back for our own trolley? Nope. Far too embarrassing. We simply walked out of the supermarket as cool as we could, leaving not one but two half filled trolleys somewhere in store. You know to be honest, Sunday morning stress free shopping is highly over rated plus I've never really liked supermarkets when they re quiet first thing in a morning anyway. They just attract weird folk.

"Right now sis, remember when we pass through supermarket security, try and look normal, ok!"

DENIAL AND THE RATS

"Maybe if I say the word delete in my head often enough this moment can be erased forever."

◆ ◆ ◆

So I arrived at Sunny Bank Farm and met the farmer Jim, hobbling out in the yard with his walking stick. I didn't want to spend too long here as I had another farm to visit.
"Right Jim, have you got all the paperwork out for me to see?" I shouted across the yard.
He looks at me astounded.
"Oh we don't bother with all that here. I've got an excellent memory lass." He proceeds to tap his head. "It's all up here," he shouts. He begins to start patting his coat pockets. "Now then, where the hell did I put that pen?"
I roll my eyes. Oh no, this means I'm going to be here forever and a day.
"Anyway the kettle is on in the kitchen and just so you know lass, we seem to have acquired a few rats at the moment. Problem is the farm cat is out of action for the time being."
"Oh don't worry about it, all farms have rats Jim."
"Oh so you don't mind them then?"
"I like all living creatures as you know Jim," I said adamantly and proudly. I have an air of superiority about me at this point. I'm hoping that I don't come across too arrogant but I respect all members of the animal kingdom.
"They all play their part," I continue adamantly, "They all play their part." He shakes his head at me in disbelief.
"What even rats?" He says astounded.
"Of course! I don't know why you're so bothered by them. They're more scared of you than what you are of them." I find myself getting carried away as he just stands there smirking at me.
"I've even considered getting some pet rats for myself actually," I lied. I just wanted to see his reaction just for the fun of it. Well he tries to wind me up often enough let me tell you.
"Well you can have mine if you want. I didn't realise you were so fond of them."
"Oh yeah, they're highly intelligent creatures actually." I raise my eyebrows as if I have profound specialist rodent knowledge. He grins back at me, speechless. I love it when that happens! It's always nice when you can get a farmer to stop talking. Admittedly though, in my experience, it's harder to stop them in their tracks if they happen to be talking about A. The weather, B. The increase in land/milk prices, C. Inheritance tax or D. All of the above. If it's D, you've no chance. You may as well stick

the kettle because you're going be there for the duration.
"I'm just outback training Luna," he shouts, "I won't be a minute."

Denial alert! Jim has no idea how to train his sheepdog, Luna. However, Luna knows exactly how to train Jim. The manoeuvres she has him doing are a joy to watch. Luna has taught Jim, 'come-by', 'away' and 'walk on.' The 'lie down' manoeuvre is usually achieved when Luna decides to run round him really fast so that he goes dizzy and topples over and then struggles to get back up with his walking stick.

I head towards the kitchen and hear the TV on. Well I say the word TV. What I really mean is TVsssssssss! He has four old TVs lined up in his kitchen so he can see what is on all the main four channels at any one time. He has told me that he likes to make use of all his old TV's but I know the real reason. It's so he doesn't have to go out and spend money on new batteries for his remote which packed in about 5 months ago. I'm not stupid!

Hey but never fear. I can top this because as said earlier, denial is what I'm good at. This is when I truly come into my own. I can make an arse of myself without even trying when it comes to denial. It's as natural as breathing. Here's how it's done!

About six months ago (it could have been longer, I try to block it out from the old grey matter) I went into a shop to buy six balls for my rescue dog as he had popped or chewed most of his. I was asked how many balls I would like. I responded,
"I'd like sex please!" Immediately I knew what I had said and just simply stood there pretending I hadn't said it. I told you, denial. I know I had said it. The person serving me knew I had said it. The **three** people in the queue behind me knew I had said it. But denial is now the only way forward. I stared back at the sales assistant without blinking and maintaining steadfast and determined full eye on eye contact. That way, I become more convincing that all is ok (denial). Maybe they will think they heard wrong (counter denial) and maybe if I say the word delete in my head often enough this moment can be erased for ever (double counter denial). I wouldn't have minded but the person serving me was at least 65, receding hairline and without their own teeth..........oh and did I mention female!

I mean it's really no different to those people who go to the chippy and get fish, chips and gravy and then ask for a Diet Coke at the end. Is this denial situation really so different? Is it? The answer is yes, of course it is. I've just asked for sex in a newsagent shop which is completely and utterly different to asking for a can of coke at the chippy but that's the beauty of denial - I can pretend it's not!

Anyway, back to the rats. Jim eventually comes into the kitchen.
"Now then, these rats. They seem to be getting in just here, from behind the Aga."
I freeze and turn to him, mouth opened wide. "You mean they are actually in the house?"
"Aye lass but you'll be all right. I think they're coming in to get warm. I thought you said weren't bothered."
"Yes but that's when I thought they'd be outside with you! Now that I'm up to speed on the fact that they enjoy dining in, things are starting to feel a tad different I can tell you." I suddenly realise that I'm no longer sounding like the devoted rat fan that I professed to be just minutes ago. So I change tactics.

"So how many are there?" I gulp. I'm trying to appear as though I'm taking all of this in my stride. I casually lean on the edge of the Aga but then realise that the rats are behind it and so ever so casually glide my arm from it. No hurry. Not quickly enough to make him think I'm scared but quick enough to avoid a pending rat attack. Have you ever tried to look relaxed and comfortable when all you want to do is run? It's not up there with your best moments. The anxiety sweats are now starting and I can tell that my breath is a tad laboured. I realise now that I'm way in over my head but my pride is stopping me from telling him that I'm terrified of rats. I mean I'm supposed to love all animals and I just said outside that rats play their part within the vast scheme of the universe. I've no idea what I meant by that and between you and me I've no idea what actual part they do play within this vast universe of ours but it sounded good at the time.

"I think it's a family of rats," he continued, "but it's only the younger ones that are coming into the house."
With some slight relief, I picture in my mind's eye, cute little fluffy type mice.
"Oh, so it's just the baby ones then?" I heave a sigh of relief.
"Not exactly," he muses. "They are more like teenage rats, you know, just daft and stupid."

See now, he says the words daft and stupid but I hear the words; brave and crafty. So these are clearly teenage rats. Now in my mind, teenage rats are likely to want to take more risks than your average adult rat. So not only are we now talking rats, we're talking unruly adolescent risk-taker rats. Oh gosh, I feel slightly nauseous. I bet there's a gang of them just hanging out behind that Aga right now as we speak with a cocky leader with trousers that hang half way down his arse!
"Anyway, you're not bothered are you?" he probed, eyeing me suspiciously.
"Bothered? Bothered? Why would I be bothered? Course I'm not bothered. I mean, after all, what are rats? They are really just glorified squirrels with tails and you know how fond I am of squirrels. No, its fine...............no problem.......................no problemoooooo." At this point, I'm stalling and saying words I don't normally say such as 'no problemo.' This is because I am now struggling to mentally process anything as the image of large rats are now invading every single brain cell that I possess. I take a deep breath.
Could this get any worse? Yes, yes it can and in fact, it does. He passes me a brush!
"Anyway, I'll leave you with this brush."
"It's a bit late worrying about a dirty floor isn't it? I think we can safely say, that ship has sailed," I snorted.
"I'm not asking you to sweep up you silly mare! It's to give 'em a quick knock on t'head when they appear."
You know, I'd actually have felt better if he'd have wanted me to sweep up. I look at him blankly. He is not smiling and I realise that he is perfectly serious.
"See now, the fact that you're not smiling actually worries me. You really think I'm going to hit some innocent creature over the head, you can think again," I snap.
"Well, fair enough lass. I'll leave you to it. Like you say, you know best. Only trying to help!"

I stare at him, baffled, as he leaves the kitchen. His wellies are off and he has a large hole in the heel of his right sock. The sun is streaming through the old, glazed kitchen window and at that very moment as he turns to leave, it beats a lazy, mocking glare onto his bare heel, as if wanting to highlight the anomaly, to make him look stupid. It works! I grin to myself. Thank you, I needed that.

He leaves and there I stand alone, in the farm kitchen. Well, obviously not completely alone as I have a whole family of vermin just behind the Aga to keep me company. I sit down at the kitchen table and begin typing. My eyes can't seem to control themselves as they constantly veer over to the Aga in the corner. I take a deep breath. Maybe if I type louder and cough a bit then it will keep them behind that Aga. This is why I am my own worst enemy. This is the moment that I cross the line between denial and actual reality. I spend the next hour convincing myself that I'm not bothered. I get my laptop out and start humming and singing away to myself. This is my conscious trying to convince my subconscious that all is well. 'I don't like Mondays' from Boontown Rats was the only tune in my head at this point. Well it is a Monday! The fact that the group is called Boontown Rats bears no relevance to this situation at all (denial). Besides maybe they are homing rats and are very loyal and friendly and Jim will end up keeping them on as pet rats. (La la land denial). The energy spent convincing myself that I'm not worried is now starting to tire me out. In short, the stress of trying not to worry is now getting to me and causing more stress.

Perhaps the cat isn't so good because it got attacked by a rather large rat? Oh I feel sick.
To make things worse, this is a very old farmhouse and so I can hear every squeak of the splintered floorboards, every creak of the ageing windows, every rattle of the old window frames and no doubt soon, the scraping and gnawing of teenage teeth and claws.

Ok let's try perspective. Yes I may have to share the kitchen with a gang of teenage rats but they are probably more scared of me than I am of them. I cough out loud just in case that theory isn't true. Oh I know, what if I stomp my feet really loud so that they know a person is here and that might scare them off for now.
So there I am loudly stomping my feet up and down the kitchen when Jim suddenly appears from nowhere and catches me.
"What are you doing lass?"
I had to think, quick!
"Er, well er………. my feet are a bit cold so I'm just trying to get some circulation you know to the old extremities." I proceed to bang my feet on the floor, stomping and flapping my arms about just for effect you understand.
"You get cold when you're just sitting down all day I insist." I'm also starting to get a bit hoarse with all the extra coughing.
"I think I might be coming down with something as well," I wheeze.
"Not the plague is it?" he grins, walking out.
You know what, between you and me, I get the distinct feeling he is enjoying this.

I'm now hoarse with all the coughing, my feet are tired from all the stomping and I've got no work done on my laptop whatsoever as I just can't concentrate. Suddenly I hear a scratching noise. I freeze, my fingers hovering over the keyboard. I hold my breath and concentrate. Nope. It's just my imagination! It's just my imagination! I realise that I'm starting to sound like the kid from the Home Alone movie but that is definitely a scratching sound. I look with dread towards the Aga. I slowly tiptoe over. Why I'm now tiptoeing I've no idea. I can now only hear the sound of my own breath and that of the scraping. I slowly reach for the brush on route. I don't know why. It just feels safer for some reason. I actually feel like I'm not breathing but I know I must be because well, I'm still alive and haven't yet been accosted by a gang of teenage rats. And then I stop. The scratching is not coming from the Aga! It's coming from the kitchen door leading to the porch. Gosh, surely they're not knocking before they come in? I thought they were teenage rats in which case they would surely just barge their way in. I could feel the sweat on the back of my neck even though I suddenly felt very cold and was nevertheless still operating in extreme slow and silent motion.

As I got nearer the door, the scratching was certainly coming from behind that door and whatever it was, it didn't sound like a baby rat. It sounded like a full grown rat. My hand hovered over the door latch as I grabbed and slowly and quietly pressed the lever down just to sneak a tiny look at what was on the other side of that door. My finger now pressed on the latch as I slowly eased the door open a tad. I saw immediately a pair of men's wellington boots on the floor by the door. My heart was pounding and the scratching was still happening. I was about to lunge toward the door with all my weight to startle whoever it was, when I was suddenly stopped in my tracks by the sight before my eyes! It was Jim! He was on all fours on the other side of the door, one hand over his mouth trying desperately not to laugh and the other scratching his nails on the door. Let me end this story by saying that the brush he gave me came in very useful and hopefully it will have taken him sometime to retrieve it.

Printed in Great Britain
by Amazon